NO SWORD FIGHTING IN THE HOUSE

by **Susanna Leonard Hill**

illustrated by **True Kelley**

Holiday House / New York

For the "Alabophilus Is My Dog" trio—turn the radio UP!
And for their equally fun-loving cousins:
Bliss, Isaiah, Calypso, Griffin, Eli, Luna, Penelope, and
Charlie (who got here just in time!)
S. L. H.

To Morgan Packard
T. K.

Reading Level: 2.8

Text copyright © 2007 by Susanna Leonard Hill
Illustrations copyright © 2007 by True Kelley
All Rights Reserved
The artwork was created using acrylic paints and pen line.
Printed and Bound in China
www.holidayhouse.com
First Edition
1 3 5 7 9 10 8 6 4 2

Library of Congress Cataloging-in-Publication Data
Hill, Susanna Leonard.
No sword fighting in the house / by Susanna Leonard Hill ;
illustrated by True Kelley.— 1st ed.
p. cm.
Summary: While jousting on cows in the backyard, Art and Lance flatten
their mother's daffodils just before the big daffodil contest.
ISBN-13: 978-0-8234-1916-6 hardcover
ISBN-10: 0-8234-1916-9 hardcover
[1. Daffodils — Fiction. 2. Humorous stories.] I. Kelley, True, ill. II. Title.

PZ7.H55743No 2007
[E]—dc22
2005052533

contents

1. The Point

At breakfast Mom said,
"You'll never guess what
the Camelot Ladies Garden Club
has planned!"
"What?" asked Arthur and Lance.
"Do tell," said Dad.
He did not look up
from *The Daily Parchment*.
"I'm all a-twitter."

"Daffodil Days!" said Mom.
"Judges will come
to all the gardens in Camelot.
Whoever has
the most beautiful daffodils
will win a one-month supply
of fertilizer!"

"Someone is in a daze,"
said Dad. "I'm not sure
it's the daffodils."
"Yeah, Mom," said Arthur.
"Have you looked behind the barn?
We have a one-*year* supply
of fertilizer!"
"That's not the point," said Mom.
"It would be an honor to win."
"When will the judges come?"
asked Arthur.
"This afternoon," said Mom.

"I'll be at the castle," said Dad.
"Every day is a busy day
   for the king."
   He got up and left.

"I'm going to run over
   to Mrs. Butterfinger's," said Mom.
"I'll see if she has time
   to fix my hair."
"The judges aren't coming to look
   at your hair," said Arthur.
"That's not the point," said Mom.
"I must look
   as nice as my flowers."

"Mom will be gone for hours,"
   said Arthur. "Let's have a war!"

Arthur and Lance climbed on
the tables and chairs and benches.
They jumped off.
They swung their swords and yelled.
They made so much noise,
they didn't hear Mom come back.

"You guys are in trouble,"
she said.
"How many times
have I told you? There is
no sword fighting in the house."

"Your hair looks nice," said Arthur.

"Nice try," said Mom.

"Mrs. Butterfinger
hasn't done it yet.
I'm going back in an hour.
Now clean up this mess!"

"We didn't break anything this time,"
said Arthur.

"That's not the point," said Mom.

"Gee, Arthur," said Lance.

"What *is* the point?"

"I have no idea," said Arthur.

2. Bad Steering

An hour later
the mess was cleaned up.
Mom was ready to go.
Before she left she said,
"Remember, boys, no sword fighting
in the house."

"What will we do?" asked Lance.

"I have an idea," said Arthur.

He went outside.

He found two long sticks.

"We'll joust," said Arthur.

"You need horses to joust,"
said Lance.

"Let's ask Gwenn
if we can borrow hers,"
said Arthur.

"We need two," said Lance.

"Dad took the horse

to the castle today."

"Hmm," said Arthur. "Let me think."

He looked around at

the chickens in the yard.

He looked at

the pigs in the pen and

the cow in the field.

"I've got it!" said Arthur.

"If we can't use strapping steeds,

we'll use strapping steers!"

"You can't mean Bossy?" said Lance.

But that was just

what Arthur meant.

"I don't think this

is a good idea," said Lance.

Arthur was not listening.

He went next door.

"Hi, Gwenn," he said.

"Can we borrow your cow?"

"Why do you want her?" asked Gwenn.

Arthur explained.

"I want to joust too," said Gwenn.

"We can take turns," said Arthur.

Gwenn brought her cow
into Arthur and Lance's yard.
Arthur got on Bossy
with one of the sticks.
Gwenn got on her cow
with the other.
"I'll be the referee," said Lance.
"Ready, set, CHARGE!"

Unfortunately, *charge* did not seem
to be a word
the cows understood.
Gwenn's cow stayed where she was
and ate grass.

Arthur's cow stepped boldly
into the daffodils.
She began eating them.
"Arthur!" yelled Lance.
"Get her out of Mom's flowers!"
"I can't!" Arthur yelled back.
"She doesn't steer!"

Gwenn and Arthur
jumped off their cows.
With Lance's help
they finally got Bossy
out of the daffodils.

"Do you think Mom's daffodils
   still stand a chance of winning?"
   asked Arthur.

"They're not standing at all,"
   said Gwenn.

"Maybe the judges will like
   flat daffodils," said Lance.

"Quick!" said Arthur.

"We'll fix them."

Arthur and Lance and Gwenn
worked hard.
They carried rocks
from the riverbank.
They brought fertilizer
from behind the barn.

They worked as fast as they could.
There was no telling
when Mom would get back.

At last they had done
all they could do.
"Do you think Mom will notice?"
asked Arthur.
Lance and Gwenn
just gave him a look.

3. The Prize

When Mom got back,
she looked
at Arthur and Lance.
"What have you done?" she asked.
"Nothing," said Arthur.
Mom went right in the house.
She looked around.
Everything was neat and tidy.
"We did not sword fight
in the house," said Arthur.

"So it seems," said Mom.

"But you did something."

Mom looked out the window.

"Oh, goodness!" she said.

Arthur was afraid

she had seen the daffodils.

"What is it, Mom?" he asked.

"Here come the judges," said Mom.

"And lots of people to watch

the judging!"

"Uh-oh," Lance said to Arthur.

"Shhh!" said Arthur.

Mom went out
to meet the judges.
"Show us your daffodils,"
said the head judge.
"Right this way," Mom said proudly.
Arthur and Lance
didn't want to watch,
but they had to see
what would happen.
The judges looked at the daffodils.
"Hmm," said one.
"Well," said another.
Mom looked at the daffodils.
Then she looked
at Arthur and Lance.
"Time to beat a hasty retreat,"
said Arthur.

Then the head judge said,
"Just a minute."
The judges put their heads
close together and whispered.

After a moment
the head judge said,
"These are not
the most beautiful daffodils,
but we have plenty of fertilizer.
We will give another prize
for the display
with the most room
for improvement."
Everyone clapped politely.

"Phew!" said Arthur.
"She can't be mad
  if she won a prize."
"This may not have been
  the kind of prize
  she had in mind," said Lance.
"Congratulations," said the head judge.
"Make good use of
  your one-month supply of fertilizer.
  It can only help."
"Thank you," said Mom.

All the people left.

Mom turned to Arthur and Lance.

She had a funny look

on her face.

"Great work, Mom," said Arthur.

"You won a prize!"

"And now I have a prize

for you," said Mom.

"Guess who gets to spread

my one-month supply of fertilizer?"

"But, Mom," said Arthur.
"You didn't say
  no jousting in the yard."
"That," said Mom,
"is entirely beside the point!"
"Oh no," said Lance.
"We're back at the point again."
"Yes," said Arthur. "There's no hope.
  We might as well
  get our shovels."